THIS BOOK BELONGS TO

PUFFIN BOOKS

Published by the Penguin Group
Melbourne • London • New York • Toronto • Dublin
New Delhi • Auckland • Johannesburg
Penguin Books Ltd, Registered Offices: 80 Strand, London WC2R 0RL, England
Published by Penguin Group (Australia), 2012
10 9 8 7 6 5 4 3
Text copyright © Davina Bell, 2012
Illustrations copyright © Lucia Masciullo, 2012
The moral right of the author and the illustrator has been asserted. All rights reserved.
Every effort has been made to contact the copyright holders for material used in this book.
If anyone has information on relevant copyright holders, please contact us.
Cover and internal design by Evi O. © Penguin Group (Australia)
Cover portrait © Tim de Neefe
Cover photograph © Rob Palmer
Printed and bound in Australia by McPherson's Printing Group, Maryborough, Victoria
National Library of Australia Cataloguing-in-Publication data available.
ISBN 978 0 14 330629 0

Poster on page 110 reprinted with kind permission from the National Library of Australia.

puffin.com.au
ouraustraliangirl.com.au

Charms on the front cover reprinted with kind permission from A&E Metal Merchants.
www.aemetals.com.au

MIX
Paper from
responsible sources
FSC
www.fsc.org
FSC® C001695

OUR
AUSTRALIAN
GIRL

Meet Alice

It's 1918 and Alice lives with her
big family by the Swan River in
Perth, while on the other side of
the world, the Great War rages.
Alice's deepest wish is to become a
ballerina, and when she auditions
for a famous dance teacher from
London, it seems her dreams might
come true. But then there is a
terrible accident, and Alice must
ask herself whether there are more
important things than dancing.

Meet Alice and join her adventure
in the first of four stories about a
gifted girl in a time of war.

Puffin Books

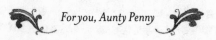 *For you, Aunty Penny*

OUR
AUSTRALIAN
GIRL

Meet
Alice

Davina Bell

With illustrations by Lucia Masciullo

Puffin Books

AUSTRALIA

1918

Northe
Territo

Western Australia

Sou

ALICE'S STORY

Alice struggles to keep her dreams of being
a ballerina alive during World War One.
Share in Alice's adventures as you read this
story of a creative Australian girl.

N

W   E

S

Queensland

stralia

New South Wales

FCT

Victoria

Tasmania

♥ Where this story takes place

0 I II III IV V VI VII VIII IX X

1
INTO THE TWILIGHT

As Alice walked out of her Friday dance class and into the wintry afternoon, she was met by two of her favourite things in the world. One was her best friend, Jilly, who had waited outside for an hour reading so they could walk home together. The other was a sunset as bright as flames. Down the hill, beyond the arch of peppermint trees that hung over Forrest Street, the air was glowing.

'Jilly, look at that!' said Alice, her face to the sky. 'Have you ever seen anything prettier?'

Jilly snorted. 'What, the sky? You've seen it

every day of your life.'

But I haven't, Alice thought to herself. Not this one. The setting sun burned like a hot, rosy ball – as red as Jilly's hair. The pink sky was streaked with gold trails like the tracks of a plough. The horizon was a purple smudge over the navy sea, and the soft night breeze smelled of salty ocean and wood fires and home. Alice rose up on her toes so she could be closer to it all, feeling her ankles twinge with the delicious ache of so much ballet.

'How was class?' asked Jilly as they set off.

'It was heaven. Miss Lillibet made us do rounds and rounds of *développés* and a new *port de bras*.' Not everyone had kept up, but Alice had loved every second. She sighed happily as she remembered the feeling – a lightness and brightness, as if she were covered in little stars. She'd felt it since she was tiny, dancing to the gramophone on the big soft rug in Papa Sir's study. And even after seven years of lessons, she felt it each time she crossed the ribbons of her ballet shoes over her ankles. Which was every day at the moment, with all the extra classes she'd been doing and practising down in the greenhouse whenever she got a second.

'Do you think Miss Lillibet will put you on pointe soon, Alice?'

'Oh, I hope so! I am still quite young, though. Perhaps I'm not good enough yet.'

'Rubbish,' said Jilly. 'You're the prettiest dancer that ever lived.'

'I wish your mother would still let you come to class – you were good too, Jilly.'

'No use wasting time wishing,' said Jilly briskly. 'I wasn't half as good as you. Besides, Mother's got some strange ideas about Miss Lillibet.'

In an instant, Alice felt her neck get hot with anger. What on earth was strange about beautiful, elegant, perfect Miss Lillibet?

'What do you mean strange?'

But before Jilly could answer, the loud clink of a bell rang out from the bottom of the hill near the Village. Alice and Jilly turned to look as a bicycle shot up towards them, past the big houses wrapped around by their shady, wide verandahs, and the big rambling gardens where cows and goats and chickens wandered. Against the sunset, the rider's curls flashed like sparks.

'Alice,' said Jilly, blushing, 'isn't that –'

'Teddy!' Alice cried. Her big brother Teddy could ride further and faster than anyone. He could pedal round Devil's Elbow with Alice and her siblings all on board and still have enough puff to sing rounds. George, who was ten and came next in the family after Alice, dinked on the crossbar, and Mabel, the next after him, sat in the big basket up the front. Little, who was six but tiny, would sit on Teddy's lap, and Alice would squeeze behind him with Pudding, their baby, who sadly wasn't a baby anymore, on her back.

'Oh dear,' said Jilly, smoothing her hair madly.

Alice smiled to herself. Jilly was always very sensible, but she went to pieces whenever Teddy was near – tall handsome Teddy with his dark tumbly hair, just like Mama's, and eyes the spit of Papa Sir's, as blue as the river, which they could see from most of their windows. Jilly wrote little poems about Teddy by moonlight, which she read to Alice when they were quite sure that they were alone. Alice would never have said so, but Jilly was not actually very good at poetry.

'Tink,' he called to Alice as he sailed past them, not even puffing. 'Look at that sunset! I'm off to the river to paint it – oh, hello Jilly. Come down – both of you,' he called over his shoulder. 'Tink, you could do your stretches there. Got to fly before it's gone!'

'Shall we?' asked Alice, as they watched him get smaller and smaller. 'Before it's too dark?'

Jilly sighed. 'I've got to do the milking.'

'Oh, of course, sorry. I'll come and help you. It's always faster with two.'

Since Jilly's papa and big brothers had gone off to fight in the Great War in Europe, she was the only one left to do the heavy chores, and her mother was terribly, horribly strict. It didn't seem fair to Alice – *her* mother didn't mind in the least about waxing the floorboards and milking Honey, their brown cow, at exactly six o'clock, and learning bits of the Bible by heart. And though Alice's father, who they called Papa Sir, had been at war for three years now, they still had Teddy to watch over them.

'No, really, it's fine,' said Jilly. 'I'm pretty quick now. Will I see you over the weekend, Alice, or do you have extra dancing?'

'Only for some of it. Come round tomorrow afternoon. Little's baked shortbread.'

Jilly looked at the ground. 'Sorry, Alice – Mother's hosting the Red Cross ladies tomorrow and I'm to take all the knitting to the depot when they've finished.'

Now it was Alice who was blushing. Peppermint Grove was filled with ladies who knitted and sewed for the soldiers, and put on fetes and balls to raise money. But since the war had started four years ago, Alice's mother hadn't stitched a sock or rolled a bandage, and everybody knew it. Mama said she didn't believe in fighting – that it all came to no good for anyone – and even when Papa Sir had gone to war, she wouldn't change her mind. Jilly's mother said that was a disgrace.

'Go and see Teddy,' said Jilly. 'You mightn't be able to for much longer.' As soon as she said it, Jilly winced as if she wished she hadn't.

Alice stopped sharply. 'You're not talking about the war, are you? You know Teddy doesn't believe in fighting.'

'Sorry Alice, I overheard Mother talking, that's all. Teddy's seventeen soon, and, well . . .'

Alice started to walk very quickly, not

minding the thump of her ballet bag against the backs of her knees. 'That's just rubbish.'

'But your father went – Papa Sir, I mean.'

'Not to fight, Jilly. He's a doctor – he went to help people, not kill them.'

Jilly looked uncomfortable.

'As if Teddy would hurt anybody,' Alice continued. 'And he's too young, anyway – you can't enlist before you're eighteen.'

'But lots of boys do and no one seems to mind,' panted Jilly earnestly, trying to keep up. 'My brothers did. And you know how people treat cowards round here – white feathers in the mail and whatnot.'

'*No*. Teddy's staying here to take care of us.'

And though it made her heart hurt to think of Jilly milking alone, the idea of life without Teddy was so unbearable that Alice sprinted off into the twilight, hoping that if she ran fast enough, she'd leave it behind forever.

2

A MILLION TINY DOTS

As Alice ran along Lovers' Walk, the path
by the river, she thought back to Teddy's
latest painting, which they'd put up on the
wall just last night. When you looked at it from
across the parlour, it was the most perfect copy
of their tall brick house with its wide verandah,
honeysuckle up the wall and the rope swing on
the ghost gum. He'd painted their tennis court
to the left, the orchard on the right, and their
bright green lawn, as big as a field, sloping gently
down to the fence line. But if you went up close
to the canvas, you could see that the whole scene

was made up of thousands of dots – millions – that seemed to shimmer like tiny coloured stars with the magic that Teddy gave them. *Castle of Dreams – Ours*, he had written underneath. Now why would he ever leave that?

'What's eating you, Tink?' asked Teddy, looking up as Alice stormed round the bend and dropped her bag next to his easel. 'Tell Uncle Ted.'

'Everything,' she said, kicking off her shoes and not knowing where to start. She found a soft patch of dirt and slid into the splits, laying her chest down and inching her fingertips towards the sliver of moon, white as milk, hanging over the water. Every night, Alice would stretch and point and glide and unfold until she felt that she had done everything that a perfect ballerina would be able to do. A *real* ballerina. It was all that she wanted to be.

Her thoughts wandered back to poor Jilly, out doing the milking. Even though Jilly's house wasn't much different to theirs from the outside, on the inside it felt a little like a church and a little like a gaol. Jilly had once told Alice that her father ran a cold bath in the evening and let it sit all night so that by the morning, when he jumped in, it was extra specially cold. Papa Sir had liked nothing better than a warm bath, a pipe and a hot cocoa all at the same time, while someone sang to him from outside the door. It's a wonder that Jilly turned out so nice, thought Alice.

'Teddy,' she said as she switched legs, 'why aren't we like other families? Not that I want to be,' she added hurriedly

Teddy paused with his brush in the air. 'There are lots of ways we're different. Which way are you thinking?'

'Well . . . how Mama doesn't really believe in things. You know, like going to church, and having a cook or a governess or anyone, and being on those committees that make things for the war – you know, like Jilly's mother does. And how she has a job.'

Mama was brilliant with numbers, and had been asked to work at a bank in Perth when the manager had left to go to war. They were all so proud of her that they didn't mind one bit that it meant extra chores. Besides, Little was magic at cooking, if someone helped her lift the pans. And even though he couldn't talk, they could always call on Uncle Bear, Papa Sir's brother who lived at the bottom of their garden with Pan, the handsomest, smiliest dog that Alice had ever met.

'Mama doesn't care what people think – she just wants everyone to do what they love,' said Teddy. 'Why do you think I paint and you dance? And Mabel sings like a blooming bird, and Little can cook like some kind of fairy chef? And Pudding, well, who knows what she'll do?'

'Love people,' said Alice smiling, thinking of their littlest sister, who was three and so blonde and plump and soft and sunny that she was always being squeezed but didn't mind a bit.

'If we were off to church or knitting socks every second, we wouldn't have time for any of that. Good grief – can you even imagine what a governess would make of Mabel?'

Alice laughed as she pictured it. Mabel absolutely could not be quiet. Mama said it was because she was eight, and that eight is a chatty age. But Alice could just imagine Mabel as an old lady, chattering away to a young man at a shop counter while people waited behind her, looking at their watches.

'As for Mama's job,' Teddy went on, 'well, she works because now she can. You mightn't remember, but before the war, women mostly stayed at home with their crochet and croquet.'

'Some still do,' said Alice, thinking of the ladies in their frilly white dresses who took tea on their verandahs every afternoon.

'Perhaps around here, where they're not

short of money. But others are working in factories and shops – there are even some at the front, driving ambulances. And the really clever ones like Mama, they're showing that they can do a man's job just as well,' said Teddy, frowning at his canvas. 'Now, is that really what was on your mind?'

Alice looked out across the mauve water to the curved white sandbar that sliced into the bay. She took a deep breath. 'Jilly heard her mother say to someone . . . that you might go and leave us. To fight, I mean.' She couldn't bear to look at Teddy, so she put her hands on the ground and flipped her legs over her head, pushing into a handstand with her body straight and strong, just as Miss Lillibet had taught her.

Teddy looked up. 'I think the real question here is whether *you're* going to leave us. They'd go wild for you in the circus, Tink.'

'Don't be funny,' said Alice crossly from upside down. 'I'm serious, Teddy. You'll be seventeen soon. Are you going to war?'

Teddy put down his palette and slowly wiped his brush on a rag, looking out at the river. 'To leave you all here alone to go off and blow up some poor fellow I've never met?' he said. 'And not be able to paint or think or see you dance again? I don't see anything brave or noble about that – I don't care that I'm one of the only chaps still here. Let them call me a coward, but you're more likely to run off and join the circus than I am to ever go to war. You have my word. Now, come and tell me if I've gone overboard on the purple.'

As she bent over his painting in the dying dusk, Alice smiled. In his tiny dots, Teddy had scooped up everything Alice loved about the river and sprinkled it onto the canvas: the way the water reflected the sky, like an echo; the tight, thin circles, like silver bangles, that formed when a bird flew by.

Papa Sir, who was from England but had

been everywhere, had told her that other rivers were brown and thin. But the Swan River – their river – was broad and wide and blue as a field of sky.

'That's why I stayed here, Tink,' he would say. 'A town on the edge of the ocean with a river like a piece of the sea.' Alice thought of him now, so far away. He would have loved Teddy's painting too.

'I think it's your best yet,' Alice said, as snuffling noises came from up the path.

Suddenly there was Pan, wagging his tail. Alice put her arms around his silky back. 'Dear Pan. Has Little sent you to call us home?'

By the time Teddy had packed up his paints, lights were twinkling across the river and the sky was deep and full with night. As they made their way up the hill, Alice couldn't help doing *jetés* – big ones – across the lawn, happy that they were home and safe and always would be, no matter what anyone said.

3

WHILE THE MUSIC PLAYS

'ARE you sure?' asked George.

'Yes! I can hear her – listen!' said Mabel.

They all tilted their heads towards the door and, sure enough, the ripples of Mama's harp were flowing from Papa Sir's study.

'Go on then,' said Alice.

George leapt up and pulled his special bundle out from behind the parlour curtains and Little fetched his map from under the sofa. Each evening, in secret, they would stick coloured pins in his big map of Europe to show where the armies were fighting. Britain's soldiers were the blue pins, and it didn't look like they were doing all that well, thought Alice, as he spread everything out.

They had to do it all in secret because Mama wouldn't have any talk of the war in the house – or anything sad or serious. *'Alors!* I will not 'ear it,' she would say in her pretty French accent. 'Life is not for worry and gloom. We must eenjoy it – every second.' But recently Alice had begun to wonder if there were some things that you couldn't pretend away – big things that you needed to think about, even if it wasn't pleasant.

As Mama played, they would listen to records while they looked at the map and went through George's war scrapbook, trying to figure out where Papa Sir might be. The first year he'd been gone, he'd sent letters and postcards every month with pictures of London and Paris, and silly rhymes and sketches.

But the gaps between letters had grown

bigger and bigger, and they hadn't heard anything now for almost a year. They used to write to him, too – every week – but one awful day before Christmas, they'd got a big packet in the mail of all their letters, tied up in string and marked 'Return to Sender'. And since then, they'd heard nothing. Mama had said it was because he was busy, and then she wouldn't talk about it again. But looking at the maps each night in secret was their way of keeping Papa Sir close to them. Somehow it helped.

'Let's have some boogie, then,' said Mabel, skipping over to the gramophone.

'Wait a second, Mabel,' said Alice. 'Where's Teddy? He hasn't disappeared again, has he?'

Nobody answered. For the past couple of weeks, Teddy had been gone at all sorts of odd times and no one knew where he'd got to.

'Oh well, we'll have to start without him. Has everyone done their chores?'

Mabel clicked her tongue impatiently. 'I've gathered up all the clothes – some people's were *very* dirty and did *not* smell good – and put them on the porch for Uncle Bear to take to the Chinese laundry. And I've got the money to pay the grocer – though we *won't* be paying for those horrid, mushy sprouts.'

Alice smiled. Mabel loved being in charge of money, and nobody could bargain with a shopkeeper quite like her. 'And Little?'

'Everything's put away in the ice chest, and I've filled the tray with more ice. The oats are soaking for our porridge, and there's stew for Uncle Bear's lunch, and I've wrapped the sandwiches in paper for school tomorrow.'

Alice looked at Little with wonder, and for the millionth time she thought that she wouldn't have believed someone so small could run a kitchen so perfectly if she didn't see Little do it every day.

'Oh, and Pudding's fed Tatty and Beaker.'

Beaker was Pudding's hen, and as jolly and pleased to see you as Pudding always was. Tatty was their grumpy billygoat who didn't do much at all.

'And I've chopped the wood and laid the fires,' said George. 'I did some calculations and I've laid the sticks at very precise angles, Alice, so that they have the best chance of catching alight.'

Mabel rolled her eyes. 'Do you *always* have to be so –'

'Oh George, I've got you a paper,' Alice said, pulling a crumpled copy of *The West Australian* out of her ballet bag. Mama didn't like them to have it in the house, so Alice kept her eye out on her way home from dancing for any copies that had been tossed away. 'And I picked some mulberries for you, Little. Also, Jilly finally gave me back *Alice in Wonderland*, so we can read a bit before bed if you'd like. Though she's still got all our Babington

Wilder books – I'll have to remind her about those. And that's all! Wind away, Mabel.'

As the music started to play and George frowned over his pins, Alice kicked off her shoes and began her stretches, thinking of what Miss Lillibet had told them that afternoon about the bones of the feet – twenty-six in all.

'Don't think I'm silly for asking, but . . . what started the war?' asked Little from on top of the piano lid, where she was sewing.

They all looked over to George for an answer, including Alice. George was only a year younger than she was, but he knew everything about everything.

'Well, obviously, it was Franz Ferdinand being assassinated,' said George, as if that settled everything.

'That means shot,' Alice whispered.

'But how did that start the war? Just one man being shot, I mean?' Little whispered back.

'Well,' said Alice, 'when he got killed, lots of people got angry – enough to start a war.'

'That's not entirely accurate, Alice. You see, Little,' said George, 'since the beginning of civilisation –'

'She won't understand that, George,' scoffed Mabel. 'She's only six.'

'Not everyone is like you, Mabel. *Some* of us care about world events.'

'And *some* of us think there's more to life than reciting very *boring* facts that –'

'See, Little,' interrupted Alice. 'England's a part of Britain. And we were settled by the English. That means that whatever they do, we do, too. You see? So when England joined the fighting, so did we.'

'Like follow-the-leader,' said Little.

'Papa Sir is English,' chimed Mabel. 'That's why he talks so toffy and nice. Like this: "Oh, I *say*! What ho! La la la!"'

'Does not,' said George. 'Does he, Alice?'

'Sort of – he does sound quite posh. I'm not sure he's ever said "la la la".'

'Has Pudding ever met Papa Sir?' asked Little. 'Where's she gone, anyway?'

Pudding popped out of the dress-up box beaming, and Alice went over and plucked her out of the nest of silk dresses to squeeze her.

'She was born after he left,' said Alice, 'weren't you, Pudding. But I'm sure she'd like him.'

'The question is whether he would like *her*,' said George without looking up from the headlines, 'given she couldn't actually say anything to him.'

Everyone turned to stare at him. George was always blunt, but Alice felt he could have been a bit kinder.

'Can too,' said Little eventually. 'Well, she could say her own words. Just not much. She's only three.'

'And you can read a whole book, and you're only six. What's wrong with her anyway?'

Pudding's trouble talking was another of the things that Mama didn't like them to mention. And as Alice kissed the top of Pudding's head and put her down, she thought that the list was getting rather long. 'She's perfect the way she is,' Alice said, settling into Papa Sir's big armchair and putting her braid in her mouth, remembering too late that eleven was too old to chew her hair.

Little came over and climbed up beside Alice to nestle in under her arm, and as Alice tucked Little's dark hair behind her ears, she felt a wave of love for her sister, so tiny and wise, like a solemn elf.

'Can I tell you a secret?' Little whispered.

'Always,' said Alice.

Little leaned in. 'I'm tired of the war.'

'Oh, Little. What makes you say that? You wouldn't remember much from before.'

'Do too,' said Little. 'I remember waving a flag when the first ones left, the soldiers. And

I remember Papa Sir. He had a scratchy beard and his eyes were smiley, like Teddy's. And he's the one what called me Little.'

'The one *who* called you Little. That's right, though. And he called me Tink.'

'Why?'

'Actually, I have no idea. Little, the war can be tiresome, but it's important, don't you think? You wouldn't want to be taken over by the Germans, and made to speak another language and eat nothing but stinky cabbage.'

'Would it be like French? I do like French.'

Because of Mama, they could all speak French, but none as prettily as Little.

'But I don't know how to cook cabbage.'

'Thank goodness for that,' said Alice. 'And one day soon, the war will be over, and Papa Sir will walk in the door and pick you up and spin you around, and everything will be all right again.'

Alice was trying to sound jolly, but the truth was she didn't know when the war would end, or if it ever would. She didn't know if Papa Sir would ever come home. All she could do was hope.

4

NEWS AND APPLE TEACAKE

'WHERE *is* Teddy?' Alice asked Mabel as she stacked up the breakfast dishes. 'I don't think I've seen him since yesterday, and he said he'd watch Pudding while I practised this morning because Mama's having a lie-in.'

'I bet he's got a girlfriend and he's off smooching,' said Mabel, 'and that's why he's never around. Think about it – he's awfully handsome and clever, and there aren't that many fellows left apart from the ones who've come back from the war, and most of them have been blown up a bit so they're not all that good-looking anymore.'

· 'Mabel! That's a horrid thing to say.' But Alice knew what Mabel meant – she, too, had seen the soldiers down at the Village with their empty shirt sleeves or trouser legs pinned where parts of them were missing, and their faces grey and old and tired. 'Besides, Teddy's going to marry . . .' Alice stopped herself just in time. 'Would you mind watching Pudding?'

'Oh – I was going to play tennis with Violet. Could she practise with you just this once? I'd take her with me, but you know what she's like with hiding the balls.'

'Of course not. Mind that you win – you're a much better player, she's just got that big serve.' Alice swept Pudding up and kissed her violently. 'Dancing, Pudding? Shall we go dancing?' Pudding grabbed at Alice's hair with her jammy hands.

'Tinker! Fifty *pliés* you'll do for that.'

The greenhouse was bright and glinty, the

leaves so green against the big panes that Alice felt as if she'd entered a secret room inside a tree, the kind squirrels might live in without anyone knowing. It had once been full of tomatoes and beans and butterflies, but Papa Sir had cleared it out and put down a wooden floor so Mama could play her harp there while she looked out at the river below.

Then Teddy had taken over the big glass room to paint, when he'd started using the smelly oils. Now one end was stacked with rags and jam jars and sheets of calico that he stretched over frames. The other end, where Alice set Pudding down, had a wide patch of floor big enough to dance across, even when you were doing giant leaps.

'Wind the gramophone, Pudding,' Alice said as she unbuckled her shoes and pulled on her ballet slippers, so soft and bendy. 'All the way round like I showed you. And then stand at the barre, ready for class.'

The barre was a clothes horse with an extra bit along the top, but it did well enough. As piano sang from the gramophone, Alice spent hours there practising her exercises with the French names that Mama had taught her to say just right: *pliés, tendues, battements, rond de jambe*.

'One-two-three, one-two-three, *balancé*, *balancé*, back-two-three, forward-two-three. That's it, Pudding! Soft arms!'

Good grief, thought Alice, as Pudding tottered back and forth on her chubby legs, frowning with concentration. There's nothing I love more than watching Pudding dance.

'Now, imagine, Pudding, that you're Anna Pavlova on stage at the Opera House in Paris.' Anna Pavlova was the most beautiful ballerina alive. Miss Lillibet had seen her dance in London and told Alice that it was so glorious, a man in a top hat beside her had wept. Will I ever be as good as that? Alice wondered, and then felt silly for even hoping.

'Don't let your fingers drop below the line of your tutu – lift them up,' she continued. 'That's the way. Now imagine *everyone* clapping, and –'

From behind them came some very loud applause, and as Alice spun around, there stood Teddy in the doorway, grinning.

'Tock!' cried Pudding, fleeing the barre to launch herself at Teddy's shins.

'Hello there, you.' Teddy hoisted her onto his shoulders. 'Sorry Tink, didn't mean to spy,' he said to Alice. 'But I bumped into someone on Napoleon Street who has something to tell you. They're waiting in the kitchen.'

'Is it your girlfriend?' Alice blurted, and then immediately wished she hadn't.

Teddy looked amused. 'You've found me a girlfriend and you didn't even tell me? Fiend!'

'Mabel said you have a girlfriend and that's why you've been sneaking off,' said Alice as they walked up through the orchard.

Teddy stopped and looked at Alice strangely.

'I haven't been sneaking anywhere,' he said quickly. 'And besides, there's only one girl for me, and she doesn't even know I'm alive, more's the pity. She's only got eyes for soldiers, just like the rest of them.' He stuck his hands in his pockets and sighed. 'Just like the whole wretched town. The war's all anyone cares about, and I'm sick of it.'

'This girl you like . . . She's not . . . She's not younger than you, is she?' asked Alice. Perhaps there was hope for Jilly after all.

'Older – twenty, same as your Miss Lillibet. Oh! Now I've gone and wrecked the surprise – that's who's here to see you.'

As they reached the side door, Teddy lifted Pudding down gently and leaned in to whisper. 'Don't tell a soul, Tink. But her name's Eleanor Eyres and she's the prettiest girl around. I'm thinking of asking if I can paint her, but I need to work up the courage.'

'That's a silly idea,' said Alice. 'I bet there

are plenty of other girls round here who'd be much nicer to paint – ones with much more interesting hair – like red hair. What's Miss Lillibet here to tell me?'

'That's a gorgeous colour, Marie-Claire – reminds me of the lawn at Regents Park,' Miss Lillibet was saying as Alice ran in. 'And apple teacake is my absolute favourite.' She was sitting at the kitchen table next to Mama, who was yawning in her green silk dressing gown. Even out of her ballet clothes, every tiny bit of Miss Lillibet was graceful and dancer-ly.

'Hello there, Alice,' she said, reaching out her long arms and sweeping Alice up to kiss her on the cheek. 'I just had to come and tell you that I've had a telegram from my old dance teacher from London, Edouard. He is coming to Australia – he'll be here in just over a fortnight.'

'That's wonderful,' said Alice. 'What for?' Miss Lillibet had often spoken fondly of Edouard Espinosa, who taught all over Europe. He had found Miss Lillibet at a dance school in England when she was only twelve and both her parents had died of the cough.

'He's coming to conduct examinations for some young dancers in Sydney and Melbourne. But –' Miss Lillibet paused to sip her tea. 'His ship is docking at Fremantle on the way. And so I've asked him if he will watch you dance there, Alice. And he has said yes to an audition of sorts. What do you say to that?'

Mama said '*Alors!*' and Alice went red. A real audition! At the same time, though . . . 'Miss Lillibet, what if he thinks I'm no good? What if I do something wrong and he thinks you're not a good teacher? Won't you be ashamed of me?'

Miss Lillibet laughed. 'Alice, I can hardly wait for him to see you. And besides, we've two whole weeks to practise. If your mother will allow it, I'll be here every day after school to rehearse with you. What do you think, Marie-Claire?'

Mama nodded. '*D'accord.* If you can keep up with your 'omeworks, Alice, you may dance until your feet fall off.'

Alice hugged herself with delight. If that's what it took to be a real ballerina, that's exactly what she would do.

'Teddy's not still around, is he?' Miss Lillibet asked.

'He was in the garden a minute ago, though he's probably disappeared again by now,' said Alice. 'Mabel thinks he's got a girlfriend. Do you want me to run and see?'

'Oh – oh, no,' said Miss Lillibet, blushing so deeply that her cheeks were almost crimson. She stood up briskly, brushing the crumbs from her lap. 'Let's start right away, shall we, Alice?' she said. 'No time like the present.'

There isn't, thought Alice as she skipped to the parlour, because this is the moment where my dream life begins.

5

A HEAVEN FULL OF DANCING

THE next two weeks whirled round Alice like a carousel of all her favourite things — more dancing than she'd ever done, stretching in the mornings, school with Jilly, frantically doing homework on the walk home. Then afternoons with Miss Lillibet preparing for her audition and her own rehearsals before she tumbled into bed. Her feet were tender and blistered, but she didn't care at all; she was in a heaven full of dancing, and nothing else mattered.

On weekend afternoons, Alice practised in

front of the parlour fire while Mabel and Little bent happily over their sewing. There had hardly been any new fabric in Miss Roberts's Drapery since the war had begun, but Mama had masses of clothes from Paris that she let them pick apart.

'*Naturellement* – of course you may. Where would I wear this now?' she would say, holding up a sky-blue ball dress or dusting off a feathered hat.

To Alice's surprise, nobody seemed tired of her ballet – not like when George recited endless facts about King Arthur, or when she had made them do the play about bears with Scottish accents. And as a special treat, Mama had learned the music on her harp. Though Alice knew Mama was tired from her work at the bank, she would play it each night as they went to bed, the warm trills floating up the staircase, as pretty as angel music.

Even Teddy, who was still mysteriously

missing for a lot of the time, made sure to ask Alice how it was all going whenever he flew in and out.

'I hope the poor fellow's wearing a helmet,' he'd say, 'because he's going to fall off his chair when he sees you.'

George had appointed himself the head of Alice's stretching routine, and he did it just right, she noticed each day, holding her legs up to her ears so that she stretched further than she thought she could, but never too far.

'We can approach this mathematically,' he'd said, 'using equations of force and distance.'

Miss Lillibet, too, was pushing Alice harder than ever before, increasing the number of exercises Alice had to do until, on the day before her audition, she couldn't feel her toes. Miss Lillibet laughed when Alice told her.

'Alice, you are ready for pointe shoes,' she said. 'Being numb with pain is what pointe is all about. I will check with Edouard – I know

you're a little young, but I'm sure he will agree.
You have the strength now, and the technique.'
She reached out to tilt Alice's chin up towards
her face. 'Alice. The way you dance . . . Well,
it's a gift, and for that we can take no credit.
But the way you work, how hard you work,
that is what *you* give. Never stop. Not for wars
or fools who will tell you it means nothing.
To dance is to bring something pure into a
world that is ugly, and more in need of beauty
than of anything.' Miss Lillibet's eyes were
starry with tears, and on seeing them, Alice's
were too. She felt suddenly older, and taller
somehow – not in her body, but inside her.

'I think it's time for a tricky question,' said
Miss Lillibet. 'I ask it of all my dancers when
I think they're ready.'

'Oh – I'm ready,' said Alice immediately.
'I definitely am.'

Miss Lillibet smiled. 'Well, then. Alice,
what is it that makes you a dancer?'

'Is it practice?' asked Alice. 'Lots of practice?'

'Ah, but what drives you to practise?' Miss Lillibet asked in return.

Alice thought for a moment. 'Wanting to be the best. Not better than everyone else,' she added hurriedly. 'Just the best for me – the best that *I* can do.'

'Excellence, yes, that's admirable. But there is something underneath our wants – every single one of them.' She nodded to herself. 'And it's love. Love is always your fuel, Alice – in life and in dancing. Each day you have been alive, it has been collecting there in a puddle, waiting to be used. What – or who – is in your puddle? There lies all you need to know about being a dancer.' Miss Lillibet fixed her bun and shook herself out a little. 'Now, I'll see you tomorrow, bright and early at half past nine. I'll drive you in the Panhard, and afterwards we'll go out for lunch in Fremantle, my treat.'

'Thank you, Miss Lillibet – for, for everything,' said Alice, suddenly feeling shy and wishing she had the words to say all that was in her heart.

Miss Lillibet tucked a stray bit of hair behind Alice's ear. 'Thank *you*, Alice,' she said. 'You've given me more than you'll ever know.'

Alice thought about what Miss Lillibet had said as she lay in bed that night, listening to the rain on the roof and snuggling under the covers. She thought of all the things she loved about ballet: not just the music and the costumes and the stories that each piece told, but the feeling that when she was dancing, she could make everything beautiful, just for a little while. She thought of Miss Lillibet, tall, young, graceful Miss Lillibet who believed so much in Alice that Alice couldn't help believing in herself.

But then came the thoughts Alice had become so good at squashing down: Was it wrong to feel most perfectly happy when across the world soldiers were cold and miserable and fighting and dying and often didn't even have socks? Was it silly to be dreaming of pointe shoes when Papa Sir might not even be breathing? It was a guilty feeling she carried around like a splinter, forgetting about it until the moment it bit and stung and took over everything.

Maybe all I can do for Papa Sir is try harder than ever, every second, she thought to herself. And hope that he would be proud.

Out Alice's window the next morning, the mist lifted off the river in curly strips, like the circles of apple skin Teddy could peel in one piece without breaking. As the crisp early sun streamed in, the windmill behind the house squeaked softly, and Alice could hear the faraway clop of the baker's cart as he made his morning rounds.

She smiled, remembering the excitement of bedtime. Mama had said the girls could stay home from school to help her prepare for her audition, and they hadn't been able to sleep with all the delight. And while Alice was at the audition, Uncle Bear was to take them for a picnic lunch, then out in the iron canoe if the weather was fine. Mabel and Little had laid out her ballet clothes with such pride and care that Alice's throat had ached. Then Jilly had come over in her nightdress to wish her well.

'I've missed you, Alice. I've barely seen you,' Jilly had said. 'And I wanted to give you something – something to wear as you danced, but then I thought that you probably aren't allowed to wear anything extra, like when you do your exams.' Then she kissed Alice on the cheek. 'There. That's my something I give you. Don't wash it off. Good luck, Alice. Not that you need it.' She paused, and tilted her head. 'When I watch you dance, I think, If I didn't know her, I would hate her for being so good. But I could never hate you. You're my very best friend.'

'And you're mine,' said Alice solemnly. 'I'll come over as soon as I'm back from my audition. I'll come over and tell you everything,' she'd promised as they hugged goodbye.

By half past eight, Alice was ready. Her ribbon, so lovingly edged and pressed, was tied around her bun. With her little white skirt she wore a dance tunic the colour of pink fairy floss, and her fingernails had been cut specially into little white crescents. Her ballet shoes were snug in her bag, wrapped up in tissue. And before Mama had left for work that morning, she kissed Alice on the forehead. '*Bonne chance* – good luck!'

From the second that Alice started swishing her feet back and forth, higher and higher, she knew that this was not going to be an ordinary day of dancing. She felt loose and light and limber. It seemed her legs were even more eager to swing than usual; her point was sharp, her legs strong, her balance sure. As Alice finished her centre work, she felt that she had danced her way to a new world, one without worry or time. She could hardly wait for Miss Lillibet to arrive at half past nine in her big, smart car – not like Rough-and-Tumble, their motorcycle with the wicker sidecar, which they loved so dearly.

'Do I have time to practise my final piece?' Alice asked George as Little changed the record on the gramophone.

'Just, I think – though it must be getting on. I'll run and check.'

But as Alice shook out her limbs a little and raised her arms to fifth position, George didn't run and check – he stayed watching her dance the best she ever had, her turns crisp, her jumps so light that her feet barely kissed the ground. When she finished, everyone applauded madly.

As Alice bobbed a little curtsey, the clock began to chip and squeak, letting them know it was quarter past ten.

It was quarter past ten, and Miss Lillibet had not come.

6
THROUGH THE RAIN

WHERE oh where was Miss Lillibet? Was she ill – but why hadn't she telephoned? Could her car have broken down? It was an hour's journey to get to Fremantle, and they would be late late late, and a dancer must never be late – Miss Lillibet had said so a hundred times.

Teddy was at school, so Alice sent Mabel out into the rain to fetch Uncle Bear.

'Uncle Bear,' she said, as he brushed water off his coat, 'could you take me to my audition in Rough-and-Tumble? I know you promised the others a picnic, but it's too rainy anyway. Please could you take me?'

Uncle Bear frowned and looked thoughtfully at the little girls, and then back at Alice. He shook his head.

'But they'll be fine on their own,' Alice said pleadingly. 'Little's practically a grown-up, and Pudding's no trouble to anyone, and Mabel's —'

'I happen to be *very* responsible,' said Mabel. 'In fact, I —'

'*Please*, Uncle Bear — I have to go to that audition. I might never have the chance again in my whole life.'

Uncle Bear hesitated, and then nodded slowly. The little girls cheered, and Alice felt she could have fainted with relief.

'Oh thank you, Uncle Bear,' she said. 'Thank you a thousand times.'

As Uncle Bear steered Rough-and-Tumble up the drive, Alice watched the rain swirl across the little white peaks of the river below. She had been dancing so deeply that she hadn't noticed the plump drops that had started to ping off the roof. Wrapped up in a raincoat with Papa Sir's top hat down over her bun, she climbed in, knowing that Rough-and-Tumble would offer no shelter from the rain that was blowing in sideways.

There was an enormous clatter, and hailstones bounced around them, like chips of hard, white peppermint. Then Little was beside them, her bare arms red with hail stings as she tried to cover her head. She opened the door and thrust an oilskin bundle at Alice's feet, saying something that Alice couldn't hear above the wind. The top hat slipped down over her eyes, and by the time her hands were free enough from the long coat sleeves to lift it up, Rough-and-Tumble was turning out onto the street, rounding Devil's Elbow with a throaty roar. Alice couldn't even turn back to see if they were waving.

By the time Uncle Bear pulled up at the steps of the town hall, Alice was sure Edouard Espinosa would have left, but she leapt out all the same. Uncle Bear leaned over, catching the tail of the coat with one hand, and reaching down to pick up Little's oilskin parcel with the other.

'What's in there, Uncle Bear?' Alice asked, but he wouldn't say anything, just nodded firmly and drove away to park.

Please, please, please, let him be here, thought Alice as she ran through the big wooden doors, looking around desperately. There was nobody in the big marble foyer, so she made for a dim corridor with doors down either side. She tried each one, crunching the handles, but most were locked. One was a closet — and as she opened it, a broom and a mop fell out with a bang. Alice jumped back with fright, and tripped on the ends of her raincoat, falling back so squarely that she bounced on her tailbone. She sat there, sad and hollow with disappointment, not knowing what to do next.

'Well, now, you must be Alice.'

Alice felt someone crouch down in front of her and lift the brim of the top hat. She looked up to see a warm, kindly face and brown eyes as lovely as any she'd seen.

'Hello, Edouard Espinosa,' said Alice, and then wondered why she hadn't said 'Mr Espinosa'. 'I'm so sorry I'm late, but you see, Miss Lillibet didn't come.'

'Oh? And where has Lily got to?' Edouard Espinosa held out his hand to Alice and helped her up. Now she was standing, Alice could see a plump lady with spectacles on a chain waiting down the hall.

Mr Espinosa saw her looking. 'Forgive my

rudeness, Alice – this is Miss Mary March. She will be playing for you today.'

'Oh! So I'm not too late? I was ready so early, and then she didn't come and she didn't call, and we didn't know what to do. And we were in Rough-and-Tumble, not the Panhard, and – oh, I'm sorry to talk so much – it's usually Mabel who can't be quiet.' Alice put her hand to her lips, feeling quite mortified.

'Not at all – it sounds like an eventful morning. Now, here's what we'll do. I'll take your coat and hat, and you change into some dry clothes, eh?'

Alice felt her whole self wilt as she wriggled out of the raincoat. 'I don't have clothes to change into. I – I didn't think to bring any.'

'Not even in your parcel?' He pointed to it on the floor.

'I don't know what's in that parcel,' Alice whispered. Good grief, Edouard Espinosa must think her the most feather-brained girl on earth.

'How intriguing! I do like a mystery. Don't you like a mystery, Miss March?'

'What I'd like is my lunch, so if you don't mind, I shall go and sit at the pianoforte before I faint dead away.' Miss March clunked off down the corridor.

Edouard Espinosa winked at Alice as he handed her the parcel. But her fingers were trembling so that she couldn't undo the string, and she had to hand it back.

'A tough little knot, that one. Ah – but what's this, Alice? Someone has given you a present. What jolly wrapping.'

Underneath the oilskin was something wrapped in the most marvellous paper, which had been drawn by Teddy, of course. It was a picture of a night sky and a dancer made of stars, making her way across the page until she finished on the edge of the paper, curtseying on the moon.

'He's done the gavotte!' Alice exclaimed.

'That's my dance – he's drawn the steps.'

'And talented he is, too – look at that beautiful turnout.'

She took off the paper carefully and peeled back the soft layers of tissue underneath. Inside was a dance tunic the colour of – well, what was that colour? It wasn't gold and it wasn't silver and it wasn't pink and it wasn't yellow, but it was a mix of all those things. And around the neckline were the most darling little feathers, so soft that it felt like you were stroking nothing at all when you touched them.

It was so familiar and yet Alice was sure she had never seen it before. She lifted it out to hold up the straps, and two cards fluttered to the floor. She recognised Little's letters – some backwards, but all tidy. *Congrautlationz!* said the first card. *It boezn't matter. we ztill love you*, said the second.

'Oh! They must have meant it for when I got home,' said Alice. 'I think they were going to choose the card that fit the best.'

'Do you think you can dance in it, Alice?' Edouard looked at his watch, and Alice remembered that he would be due back on the ship soon.

She nodded, and he left her to change. Her ballet tights were still damp – her ribbon too – but the new tunic felt so heavenly that she hardly noticed.

Then suddenly Alice realised why it seemed so familiar – the fabric, and the feathers. It was Mama's wedding dress, cut small, just for her.

As Alice climbed the stairs and stepped out onto the stage, she felt the spring in the boards under her toes, and smelled the musty scent of heavy curtains – real theatre curtains. The up-and-down rows of seats stretched before her like a rippling sea. When the lights came up, Alice felt like a butterfly unfolding into the sunshine. She forgot that Miss Lillibet wasn't there. She forgot everything except how much she loved to dance.

'Let's get started then,' Edouard said, taking the lid off his fountain pen and pulling out some paper. 'Thank you, Miss March – the *battements tendus*. Aaaaand one-and-two-and-three-and-four-and.'

In her costume with the feathers, Alice had never felt more graceful. Just as it had this morning, each tiny movement felt perfect. Her barre work ended with an arabesque that gave Alice the feeling of closing a wonderful book. She smiled down at her feet, not wanting Edouard to think she was being immodest.

'Splendid, Alice!' he said. 'Has Miss Lillibet talked about putting you on pointe? You're more than ready.'

'Oh!' Alice looked up. 'She meant to ask you today. Do you really think I could?'

'Those feet were made for pointe shoes,' he

said. 'And who would have thought that such small ankles could be so steely, eh? You must have put in some hours on those.'

By the time she got to her performance pieces, Alice had forgotten about doing her best – it seemed that today she couldn't do anything else. As she sprang and leapt and stretched and fluttered, she found her thoughts wandering back to Miss Lillibet and all the times they had spent together. She thought of Pan's wide, happy mouth, and Uncle Bear's big heart. And the way Mabel talked all in a rush because she just couldn't wait to tell things. How Alice felt when Teddy winked at her or when Pudding nuzzled her neck, and how carefully George pulled her arms behind her to stretch between her shoulder blades. She remembered Papa Sir, his pipe and his crinkly eyes, and the kiss on her cheek from Jilly, which she still hadn't washed. She thought of Mama, so strong and stylish and fierce and French. And of Little, precious Little, so delicate and kind.

And all at once, Alice realised that she had begun to dance from love. If only Miss Lillibet had been here to see what she had made from her very own puddle.

As she finished her final dance in a curtsey that brushed the ground, there was wild applause. But it did not come from Edouard Espinosa, who was scribbling furiously.

'I don't usually look up from the pianoforte when I'm accompanying,' said Miss March as she finished clapping, 'but today I couldn't help it. Ducky, that was glorious.'

'Thank you, Miss March. Your playing was lovely too,' Alice said, as she bounced down the steps.

But Edouard Espinosa did not look up as she approached. He just kept writing, frowning a little. Oh dear, thought Alice. Had she been enjoying it all too much and not been concentrating – had she been sloppy?

'Alice,' said Edouard slowly, still writing. 'Have you ever seen Lily – Miss Lillibet – dance?'

'She does a dance every year at our end-of-class concert.' Alice sighed, thinking of Miss Lillibet turning pirouette after pirouette, as if she were a figurine in a music box. Last year she had worn a long white skirt that had flowed around her like a puff of mist.

'I first saw her when she was about a year older than you.' Edouard finished writing with a flourish, and blew on the paper to dry the ink. 'I was captivated. She was so young, and yet . . .' He wiggled the paper into a big cream envelope. 'And yet she seemed to dance with an old soul, one that had known great sadness and made it into great beauty.'

Oh no – there I was being so smiley, thought Alice.

Edouard Espinosa licked the envelope shut

and put it down. He clasped his hands together and looked up at Alice thoughtfully.

'Now, your technique is just as good as Lily's was then – better even. Your training has obviously been exemplary. But when I watched you dance . . .' He paused and looked up at the ceiling, frowning.

Just say it, thought Alice with a sinking heart. Say I'm not nearly as good.

'When I watched you dance, your joy was even more beautiful.'

Behind them, Miss March cleared her throat. 'I shall be waiting with the driver, Mr Espinosa. We're due back at the ship smartish. Goodbye, dear, and all the best.'

As Miss March clipped out on her little heels, Alice scrunched up her courage to ask what she had really come to find out. 'Mr Espinosa,' she said to the floor. 'I know you have to go, but before you do . . . can I ask . . . Do you think, one day, maybe, there's the possibility that, if I worked so, so hard, and practised every day, perhaps, just perhaps, I could be a real dancer?'

Edouard put his pen in his bag and picked up his hat and coat. He stood up and came around to Alice and knelt so that she could see right into his kind, brown eyes.

'Alice,' he said gravely. 'I have never seen a dancer as real as you.'

He held out the envelope. 'When you find her, please give this to Lily with my regards, and make sure she reads it. I'm sorry that I can't stay longer, but I have no doubt our paths will cross again.'

7
MEANWHILE

SHOULD I have changed out of my dance clothes? Alice wondered, as she waved goodbye to Uncle Bear and skipped across the tennis court to Jilly's house next door. But she so wanted Jilly to see it that she decided not to go back and change.

She pushed back the boards in the side fence and slipped cautiously through the honeysuckle. As she ran up through the McNairs' kitchen garden, she couldn't help but do flying leaps, so that by the time she reached the side door she was puffing. She knocked impatiently and pushed her nose up against the window.

Eventually Jilly's mother appeared, and Alice stepped back, wishing she hadn't smeared the glass. Mrs McNair strode towards the door with her eyes squinted up and her lips pushed together so hard they were white.

Before the door was all the way open, before Alice could open her mouth to ask for Jilly, Mrs McNair was spitting words at her.

'Have fun doing your *dancin'*, did you? Playin' at nonsense with that German lass while the rest of us do our bit for the war?'

German lass? 'I don't know any –'

'Aye, you should be *ashamed*, prancin' round in something like that when there's fam'lies with nought on the table.'

Alice looked down at the wedding-dress tunic shimmering in the afternoon sun.

'But we shouldnae expect any different, given who your mother is – her off pretendin' to be a man, fiddlin' with numbers and actin' clever while her children run round like spoilt mongrel *dogs*.'

Alice took a step back.

'And *cowardly* mongrel dogs at that! Aye – that brother o' yours, hidin' away with his paints because he's too afraid to fight. He makes me *sick*.'

'But Teddy's too young to go fighting!'

'Pfffft – tosh. My Hamish was off at fourteen. And Douglas signed up the first chance he could when it all began, and he weren't a day older than your precious Teddy is now. So *don't you dare* be sayin' he's too young when the truth is that he's nigh seventeen and plain disgustin'. What a fam'ly – cannae even talk, the half o' you.' She leaned in closer and smiled in a way that was not friendly, little bubbles glistening on the edge of her lips.

'And now see what you've done,' she said quietly. 'You've killed that little 'un – the only decent one o' the lot. Drowned, and because of you and all this foolishness. Aye, that's right – left all alone, and see what happened? Blue she was, by the time they pulled her out o' the river. I saw her m'self, carried across the lawn like a broken doll.'

Alice gasped. 'What do you mean? What are you talking about?'

'You heard what I said,' sneered Mrs McNair. 'And I doubt you'll ever sleep a solid night again – nor should you. Now, some of us have work to do. *Good day*,' she said, and slammed the door.

As Alice ran back through the kitchen gardens, her eyes were blurry. She didn't see the clump of lettuces that snared her ankle, tossing her into the mud. She picked herself up and wriggled awkwardly through the hole in the fence. Her tights snagged on a splinter and tore. By the time she got to the kitchen door, she didn't have the breath to call out. She stumbled in and leaned heavily on the kitchen table to catch it.

It couldn't be true – Pudding couldn't be dead. Mrs McNair was just being horrid. Wasn't she?

And yet . . . hadn't the littlies been left alone? And hadn't they been looking forward so much to the ride in the iron canoe? Hadn't the wind been strong – strong enough to tip over a boat? And hadn't Uncle Bear left them because of Alice – because she had begged him – because she had been dancing? Alice put her head on her arms and closed her eyes.

Mrs McNair was right. It was all her fault; she knew it in her heart. Oh, Pudding . . . round, sweet, sunny Pudding. Alice felt a cold stillness in her chest, as if it had been cased in stone. She never even got the chance to learn to speak, thought Alice sadly. Because of me, she'll never know what she was good at. And all because I wanted to dance.

'Tink?' came a little voice right next to Alice's ear. 'Tink?'

Alice's snapped her head up and there was Pudding, grasping Alice's leg with her pudgy hands.

'Pudding! Pudding – you're alive. Come here, you scamp – oh, I knew it couldn't be true.' Alice knelt and pulled Pudding's downy head under her chin and squeezed her solid little body until Pudding wriggled and squeaked. 'Sorry, Baby, sorry, but I thought you were gone.' Pudding offered Alice the bottom of her dress and Alice took it, wiping at her wet, hot cheeks.

'Alice?' whispered Mabel from the doorway. 'Alice, did you hear? Something has happened. You need to come upstairs. Little might be dying.'

8

THE HAZY DUSK

'AND I know we shouldn't have done it, Alice, but we did and everyone was having a lovely time. Then a big gust came and Little was tying my pinny to the front of the canoe like a sail and the wind took it and she reached out to catch it and then she went over the edge. And she was so tiny she didn't even make a splash, so we couldn't see where she'd gone, and I dangled my oar for her to catch, but then it dropped. And when they found her, she'd got lost under the boat and sunk to the bottom before she could breathe again.'

Mabel was still whispering, but she needn't have bothered, Alice thought, because Little couldn't hear them. They had pulled chairs up close to her bed, where she lay, grey and crumpled, her lips as dark as if she'd been stealing mulberries. Her arms had been folded across her chest and in the dim evening light they glowed like crossbones. Alice watched for the rise and fall of her chest so closely that her eyes burned. Dr Peters had said it was all they could do – watch over her and wait.

'Where's Mama, Alice?' asked Mabel.

Alice wished she knew. They had been waiting for her all afternoon and into the hazy dusk. Teddy had even used the telephone to call the bank when he'd got back from wherever it was that he went these days, but it turned out that Mama had left long ago.

Eventually Teddy, tired with pacing, had ridden off into the night to find her, and Uncle Bear had taken Rough-and-Tumble down to the station in case she had caught the train. Now night had fallen and she still wasn't home and she might be too late, because Little's breaths were becoming slower.

Didn't Mama care that they were all alone? Alice wondered angrily.

George came in, clutching one of Papa Sir's weighty medical encyclopaedias. 'Been doing some research, and it's not looking good, I'm afraid. According to this, being starved of oxygen could have affected her brain by now, or damaged it. Possible outcomes include death, severe –'

'Shut *up*, George. You heard Dr Peters – he said she might be fine,' said Alice.

'Or that she might never wake up,' said George matter-of-factly. 'I'm just telling you the science. Shame Papa Sir isn't here, that's all I can say.' George closed the fat book and leant over Little, kissing her forehead tenderly. 'Goodnight Little.'

Alice had been thinking about Papa Sir all afternoon, wishing that he were here. Perhaps, just perhaps, he could have fixed Little. Perhaps he could have made everything all right again.

When Teddy returned, Pudding was asleep on Alice's lap and Mabel at her feet.

'Did you find her?' Alice whispered.

Teddy shook his head, looking tired and sad. He didn't say anything, just gathered Pudding and Mabel into his arms and carried them off to bed. Alice put her cheek next to Little's and closed her eyes. Her head ached and her stomach churned.

'Go and get some sleep, Tink,' Teddy said when he came back in. 'I'll come and find you if anything happens. I promise.'

If it had been anyone else, Alice wouldn't have believed them; she would have stayed watching, just in case. But Teddy always kept his promises. She held out her arms and he lifted Alice up as easily as if she were made of cotton, and carried her to her room. Teddy tucked her gently into bed, but as he tiptoed away, Alice noticed something strange. Was it real, or was she already dreaming?

'Teddy?' Alice whispered into the darkness. 'Why are you wearing those soldier boots?'

But the door clicked shut, and Alice fell back on her pillow, feeling her eyes slide shut.

Alice awoke at that peculiar time between first light and sunrise when the sky is all milky. The mud was gone from her palms, but she was still wearing her dance clothes and the sick feeling was still with her. From beside her bed, she heard somebody yawn. She looked down to see Mama, curled up under an eiderdown on the floor, watching her. Alice felt a rush of love and surprise, but it quickly turned to anger.

'Mama, where were you?' she asked. 'Why

didn't you come home? We needed you.'

'*Bonjour, ma petite*,' Mama whispered, sitting up. '*Ça va?*' She reached out and stroked Alice's hair.

'*Ça va*,' Alice whispered back crossly. But that wasn't how she felt at all, and the gentle touch of Mama's hand made her eyes fill with tears.

'I was 'eld up. There have been . . . some troubles.'

Alice sniffed and closed her eyes, scrunching them shut against the question she had to ask. 'Little . . . is she . . .?'

'She is still sleeping but 'er breathing is stronger. Dr Peters came by again in the night. He says we must wait. Teddy is there.'

'*Maman* . . .' Where should she start? '*Maman*, it's all my fault, because Miss Lillibet didn't come, and then I made Uncle Bear take me to dance.'

Mama bit her lip and looked away, not saying anything.

'Mama?' Alice tried to sit up. 'It was my fault, wasn't it? That's what you think, too!'

'*Non non non, ma cherie.* Not at all. It's just that . . . I 'eard some news yesterday . . .'

Suddenly Alice remembered what Mama had said about there being troubles.

'. . . while I was at the bank . . . all day people were talking, and I am thinking at first *c'est pas vrai* – it isn't true. So after work, I went to 'er cottage, and then to see Ginger . . .' She swallowed, tracing Alice's ear with her finger. Ginger was what everyone called Constable Jenkins, their policeman. Why on earth had Mama been to see him?

'Whose cottage?' asked Alice. 'And why did you go to the police?'

'Miss Lillibet's. She 'as been taken away. I went to try and find where she is being kept.'

Alice couldn't believe what she was hearing. 'What do you mean, taken away?'

'To a camp . . . an internment camp.

Because Germany is our enemy in the war, lots of German people 'ere are being locked away in camps like prisons.'

'But Miss Lillibet isn't German! She's English.' Alice lay back, relieved. 'It must all be a mistake.'

'*Non*, but 'er grandfather was German, and these days, the world is so 'orrible that this is enough to be put in gaol.' Mama sighed. 'You know how suspicious people are now.'

That's what Mrs McNair had meant when she said 'that German lass', Alice realised.

'When people feel powerless,' Mama continued, 'they look for enemies all around them, *non*? She is lucky, I suppose, that she was not taken sooner. I am sorry, *ma petite*.'

Alice tried to imagine Miss Lillibet in a dirty prison camp in her long, white cloud skirt. She knew about the camps for German people – there had been one on Rottnest Island for a while. And the kind old Schultz brothers who lived at St Just, the house up the road, had been sent to one in New South Wales. People had thought they might be spies, signalling to German ships from their balcony.

Alice sighed and looked up at the pattern on her ceiling. If I hadn't been dancing, Little would be awake now, stirring the porridge, she thought. If I had been helping do things for the war instead of all that practice, none of this would have happened.

Miss Lillibet had told Alice never to stop dancing – that the world needed beautiful things. But suddenly Alice didn't find her dancing beautiful. She found it selfish and ugly. Mrs McNair was right: Alice had no business prancing around when so many people were suffering.

Alice looked down at her lovely dance clothes, and sat up with a start, suddenly remembering. 'Mama, my new tunic – it's your wedding dress,' she said. 'Oh, Mama. You shouldn't have cut it up – it's too beautiful for me. You should have kept it to remind you of Papa Sir.'

Mama frowned and stood up quickly. 'I must go and check on Little. Sleep some more, if you can.'

As she closed the door behind her, Alice began to cry, silently at first but then louder. How were they to remember all the nice things about Papa Sir when Mama would hardly even let them say his name? And what was the point of loving people if you were only going to lose them?

Alice felt a big hate well up in her heart. She hated Mama, she hated the war, she hated that Papa Sir was gone.

But most of all, she hated herself and the dancing that lived inside her.

9
JUST A DREAM

THAT morning, Mama didn't go off to the
bank and Alice wondered if she might
have decided to stay home forever to take care
of them. In the days that followed, though, she
went back to work and didn't come home each
night until after they were all in bed. As far as
Alice could tell, she barely looked in on Little. It
was as if she wanted to pretend that nothing was
happening. It made Alice burn with anger.

They didn't go to school that week, and
nobody answered the knocks of the people
who called by – nobody wanted to look into

their kind, sorry faces. Jilly left a pot of soup on the back porch with a lovely note, but when Alice thought of going over to thank her, it felt too hard; she felt too tired. For three days and three nights, they did nothing but take turns waiting by Little's bedside.

George read to Little from the poetry of Alfred, Lord Tennyson.

'Break, break, break
On thy cold gray stones, O Sea!
And I would that my tongue could utter –'

'Good grief, George – you'll kill her with boredom,' said Mabel.

'Mabel! That's a terrible thing to say,' said Alice.

'Well, it's true – I've been singing her show tunes, and she much prefers it, I can tell.'

Pudding wound up Little's music box over and over until the key bent and it wouldn't work anymore. Alice lay next to Little, smoothing her hair and hoping that somehow the warmth and life in her own body would skim the bed sheets and enter Little's. Teddy just sat with Little's hand in his, as if he were cupping flakes of gold.

Sometimes she stirred and once her eyelids flickered, but Little did not wake up.

With all that had happened, nobody had thought to ask about Alice's audition, and she was glad of it. But on the fourth day, Alice remembered what Edouard Espinosa had given her. Leaving George with Little and *Eighteenth Century British Verse*, she wandered round the house, eventually finding Papa Sir's raincoat mashed in a ball by the kitchen dresser.

Alice reached into the deep pocket and pulled out the envelope that was addressed to Miss Lillibet. She held it in her hands, unsure of what to do next. It wasn't right to open someone else's letters. But who knew when

Miss Lillibet would return to read it herself? Does it even matter what's inside? Alice asked herself. Do I even care anymore?

But she did. Of course she did. Alice slipped the letter down the front of her pinafore and called to Pan, who came bounding happily from in front of the parlour fire. She ran to the greenhouse and threw herself onto the wooden floor, her heart clunking.

'Should I really open it, Pan? Even though it's addressed to Miss Lillibet?' Pan wagged his tail and so Alice pulled open the envelope with her finger and unfolded the letter. She cleared her throat. 'I'll read it to you. It says . . .

'My dearest Lily,
'You told me that Alice was talented. But this couldn't have prepared me for what I saw this morning. Without question, Alice is the most gifted dancer I have seen. In fact, I suspect that she may go on to be the most famous, most glorious dancer of

our times. Under your tutelage, she has developed exquisite technique. But we both know that a true ballerina like Alice is more than that.'

Alice stopped, feeling herself blush. Even though Pan was just a dog, she felt strange saying all these things aloud.

'When the war ends, God willing, I am determined to start an academy in London. It would be my honour to be entrusted with the care of Alice. The chance to see theatre, opera and the arts; to travel to the Continent and work with the best choreographers – this would be just the beginning. I am quite overcome with excitement, and wish that I could go myself and rip the guns from the hands of every soldier if it would hurry along this tiresome conflict.

'If you wish to accompany her, Lily, you know you are always welcome in the home of your good friend,

'Edouard.'

'Woof,' said Pan, grinning.

Alice eyed him warningly. 'Pan, it doesn't mean anything, so don't go acting all happy.'

But even though she'd tried to squash down her hunger for ballet, Edouard Espinosa's letter had made it roar inside her once more. Before she knew what she was doing, she was over by the gramophone. It's a pity I don't have my shoes, she thought. Perhaps I could sneak up to the house without anyone seeing and . . .

She stopped.

Wherever Miss Lillibet was now, she certainly wasn't dancing. And up in the house, because of her dreams, Little lay slowly dying. Though Alice's love of dance felt as wide as the sky, her love for Little was as big as a galaxy. She realised that there was nothing – *nothing* – that she wouldn't do to have Little back.

'If Little wakes up,' she said, 'I'll never be selfish again. I'll knit a thousand socks – a million. And I'll help Jilly roll bandages and

I'll . . . I'll give up ballet forever. If she comes back to us, I'll never dance again. I promise.' She wasn't just talking to Pan – she was talking to something bigger: to the world, or perhaps even to God, though she didn't know him well enough to be sure.

She folded up Edouard Espinosa's letter to throw on the fire later. She pulled the leather cover over the gramophone and pushed the clothes-horse barre into a corner.

'Woof,' said Pan suddenly, his ears pricked. 'Woof,' he said, and wagged his tail madly.

'I don't know what you're so pleased about.' Alice sighed. 'It's not like there's anything nice left in the world.'

'ALICE,' cried Mabel, throwing open the door and making Alice jump. 'You have to come now – it's happened!' And then she turned and fled.

What did she mean – what had happened? Alice wondered as she chased Mabel up to the house. She'd been in and out so quickly that Alice hadn't seen her face. And her voice, loud and desperate, could have been happy or sad.

Either way, Alice knew that it was Little's bedroom where the thing had happened. As she raced there and stood outside the door, she felt she could have outrun a tiger.

Squashed into Little's pretty yellow room were George and Mabel, Pudding and Mama, Teddy and Uncle Bear. Everyone was silent. Their eyes were fixed on Dr Peters, who was bending over the bed so Alice couldn't see past him. What was he looking at?

Finally he moved aside, and Alice gasped.

'Hello, Alice,' said a little voice. 'I was wondering where you were.'

'Hello,' said Alice uncertainly, pinching herself to prove it wasn't a dream.

'Aren't you very pleased to see me?'

'Oh, Little, of course I am.' Alice rushed forward and squeezed Little's shoulders. 'It's just that – I was in the greenhouse – and then only a minute later . . . never mind. I've missed you so much.'

'It feels like I've been asleep forever,' said Little when Alice finally released her. 'Have I missed Teddy's birthday?'

They all looked at each other in surprise. With everything that had happened, they'd all forgotten that Teddy would be seventeen – when? Tomorrow?

'You haven't, Little. We're having a high tea,' Alice decided on the spot. 'And you'll be the guest of honour. Besides you, Teddy, of course – but you don't mind sharing, do you?'

'This second, I don't mind anything at all,' he said, gazing at Little.

'It is very nice to have you all here, but would you mind if I had a rest?' Little asked.

'But you've been asleep for three days – four almost. How incredibly boring. Don't you want to get up and skip around a bit?'

'Mabel!' they all said together.

'*Dors bien* – sleep well, Little,' said Mama, shepherding everyone out of the room. 'Alice will tuck you in.'

As Alice smoothed the sheets, Little looked up at her with wonder. 'When I was asleep, I dreamed that you were dancing,' she said, 'on the stage in London, like Anna Pavlova. And when I woke up, Alice, I knew that one day it will come true.'

'Hush, Baby,' whispered Alice, turning out the light and kissing Little on both pale cheeks. 'It was just a dream.'

And that, thought Alice sadly, is all it ever will be.

She had Little back and, just as she'd promised, she would never dance again.

10
A SPECIAL DELIVERY

MABEL, George and Alice looked at Teddy's birthday cake with dismay.

'I don't know how this happened,' said George glumly. 'According to the rules of physics, the combination of temperature and ingredients should create a *rising* effect, not this . . . crater.'

'The middle's sunk – we don't need science to figure that out, George. And my jam tarts are all leaning to the left and burned on one side,' said Mabel, sighing. 'How does Little make everything so perfect?'

Alice felt weary. 'We'll fill the hole in with icing,' she said. 'Teddy won't mind.'

The preparations for Teddy's birthday high tea had not gone well. The kitchen looked like Pan and Pudding had been let loose in there together. There was a gritty layer of flour underfoot, and every pan and tin was filled with batter or crumbs. Not once but twice Mabel had burned her hand, and she and George had fought over the silliest things.

Alice had found it hard to concentrate – she'd kept running up to Little's bedroom in a panic. But Little was there each time, awake and reading, puzzled by all the fuss.

'I'm still here, Alice, and I don't need anything,' she said on the sixth visit. 'Are you sure you wouldn't like me to come and help?'

'No, no, no – you heard Dr Peters. You're to stay in bed and rest until you're strong.'

'But I was never strong in the first place,' said Little, 'and it's lonely here by myself.

Do you think they'll let me up for the tea?'

'If they don't, we'll have it right here, around your bed. Though I'm warning you, our food isn't a scratch on yours. Turns out the rest of us are oafs in the kitchen.'

But it wasn't all bad. Alice's scones turned out nicely, and there was Little's jam, and some buns that weren't too hard. They laid the best china tea set out on the big dining table, and by the light of the fire, crackling merrily in the corner, it all looked delicious. Around the room, Alice had put seventeen candles in jars and teacups so everything twinkled.

As she lit the final one, they all arrived at once: Uncle Bear with Pudding on his shoulders, Mama back from the bank, Mabel and George jostling with the presents, and Teddy, cradling Little in his arms. Her pixie face seemed thinner, her eyes bigger, but as Teddy sat her next to him at the head of the table, her face shone.

'Before we start the tea, we have a special delivery for Teddy,' said George, pulling a large envelope from behind his back. Alice wondered what it could be – they hadn't discussed this bit at all.

Mabel beamed. 'It doesn't say who sent it, but it must be Papa Sir, mustn't it! And we kept it as a surprise, even though George said I would give it away, but ha! I didn't, and that just goes to show . . .'

As Mabel chattered on, Alice thought her heart would burst. Papa Sir! Was he coming home at last?

Teddy ripped open the envelope, grinning. Inside was a piece of thick card. The first side was blank. But as Teddy turned it over, two white feathers fluttered to the floor, and everyone fell silent.

'Why would Papa Sir send you those?' Mabel demanded after a long pause. 'Don't white feathers mean that – mean that . . .' She looked uncomfortable. Alice was sure Mabel knew what white feathers meant. Since the war had begun, there had been endless stories about them turning up in boys' post boxes. Boys who didn't want to go to war. Alice looked over at Teddy, who had gone very red. How dare they, she thought. Oh, Teddy.

'They mean that I'm a chicken – a coward. For not joining up.' Teddy's voice had started to shake. 'They mean that I'm weak.' He looked down at his plate.

'No!' said Alice. 'Don't let them make you think that, Teddy!'

'They're right,' he said. 'I have been a coward. But they needn't have bothered with the feathers, because I've already decided.' Teddy took a deep breath and looked up, straight into Mama's eyes. 'I'm not twenty-one yet, so you'll need to come with me to sign the forms, *Maman*. Because I've made up my mind – I'm going to fight.'

Alice felt as if she'd been hit in the stomach while she was looking the other way. 'But you promised,' cried Alice. 'You promised you would stay here and protect us! When we were down at the river – remember?'

Teddy looked at Alice and then down at Little. 'Even when I'm here, I can't stop bad things from happening. At least if I'm over there fighting, I'll be doing something to keep you safe.' He swallowed. 'And besides, I can't take it anymore – the shame of not going. I'm no use to you here if I'm hiding away because I can't look anyone in the face. It brings disgrace on the family.'

'No one cares about that,' Alice said with tears in her voice. 'If you leave, I'll never forgive you, Teddy.'

'Well, I am leaving – shipping out to the camp at Blackboy Hill first thing on Monday. That's what I've been doing these last weeks – learning to shoot and getting my boots and having the medical check-up. I'm sorry, Tink, that I'm going back on my word. But things change. It's the right thing to do.'

Mama thumped her fist on the table. 'To go and fight for England – a country you have never seen? And for what? To prove you are not afraid of death? *Mon fils* – my son – everyone is afraid of death! That is 'ow we know we are still alive. And you will be most alive 'ere, with your family, not rotting in some trench.'

For once, Mabel had nothing to add, and George didn't have a fact to fill the silence.

'Gone,' said Pudding into the candlelight.

'*Oui*,' said Mama, and sighed. 'But not forever. Teddy, I am not 'appy with your choice, but it is yours to make – I have raised you to have your own mind, all of you. And so, *oui*, I will sign the forms.' She reached across the table for Teddy's hand. '*Bonne chance, mon fils* – good luck, my son.'

11
THE LAST SUNDAY

THE next day was Sunday, but it didn't feel like Sunday at all. Everyone was quiet and mooching around – even Pan. Alice's face felt raw from crying and she hadn't spoken a word to Teddy since supper. It made Mama exasperated to see them so glum.

'*Alors!* Such moping. Out, out, out! Take a picnic somewhere, far away from me.'

As Alice packed up the basket, her jaw was clenched tight with anger. Of course Mama wants us out, she thought darkly, so she can pretend nothing's happening.

It felt like springtime already as they walked out into the high, bright sunshine. A little breeze tugged at their hats and bonnets. Soon the freesias would cover the banks like thick icing, and the lawns would be dry and prickly. The dusk would be long and perfect for outside games that only ended when you couldn't see through the darkness. But what would be the point if Teddy wasn't there?

They spread out their things under the elm at the bottom fence. No one said much, but by the time they got to the lopsided jam tarts, things didn't seem quite as bad.

After lunch, Mabel and George hitched Tatty to their billycart, and took the little girls for rides. Alice felt restless, wanting to stretch and jump and glide. But she couldn't now.

'Fancy a dip, Tink?' said Teddy, putting down his book.

Alice turned her head away and sniffed, but he pretended not to notice.

'It'll be chilly, but we won't mind, will we? I brought our costumes, and we needn't tell the others exactly where we're going. I'll race you to the sandbar. What do you say?'

Alice shrugged. It wasn't ballet, but it was something.

'Be back in a bit!' Teddy called to the others as they sprinted down the hill.

They changed quickly among the bushes into their neck-to-knees, and walked to the end of the boatshed jetty, away from the baths where ladies and gentlemen had to swim separately. Alice stood back as Teddy launched himself in. She loved the way he dived with his arms out, waiting until the very last second to bring them back together. There were so very many things about Teddy that she loved, and as he sliced the water elegantly, she realised that she was ruining their last day together – maybe the last day they'd ever share.

The chill of the river bit at Alice, so that by

the time she got over to the sandbar, she was panting. Teddy was already lying at the edge of the water, almost dry. She flopped down beside him and watched gold streaks dance over her eyelids as she tried to get her breath back to tell him she was sorry.

But when she sat up, Teddy had wandered towards the shore and was only a speckle. And then Alice couldn't see him at all – only his footprints, like a trail of little memories in the sand.

Alice hunched into a ball and closed her eyes to the thought of it, feeling herself grow colder and colder as the breeze picked up.

And then Teddy was lifting her up and sitting her on his knee. It made Alice ache to feel the comfort of him. She almost wished she'd never known it, so that it didn't hurt so much to lose. Eventually she looked up, and saw that his thoughts were far away. Perhaps they were already in another country, far from her, far from home.

'You won't know this, Tink,' he said after a while, 'because Mama will never talk about these things. But she had another baby before you – a little girl. She was called Juliette and she was very, very small.' He swallowed. 'I was three when she was born, and if I sat really still on the settee, I was allowed to hold her.'

'Another baby? As small as Little when she was born?' Alice turned to look at Teddy with wonder. She remembered Little's tiny arms, smaller than Papa Sir's thumbs.

'Maybe even smaller, though I don't s'pose by much. But she died when she wasn't very old. She got a fever, and everyone was so sad. Papa Sir cried and cried. And Mama wouldn't talk about it – not a word. From then on, she would never speak about things that were sad.'

Alice felt as if she suddenly understood a great many things; as if Mama was a map she had been reading upside down. She felt her anger slide away.

'So when *you* were born,' said Teddy, 'you were all the more precious – the most precious thing in the world. Papa Sir would hardly let you out of his sight – it was all Mama could do to get him to leave the house without you. And I would talk to you for hours and hours, Tink, and sit you on my knee, just like this.' He squeezed Alice close and Alice felt that something inside her remembered those hours, even if she couldn't quite picture them. 'You'd think I'd have minded that everyone seemed to love you best, but I didn't. You made us all so happy.' He sighed. 'You *make* us so happy. Like a marvellous glue that holds us together. That's what you are. I'm saying all this . . . well, I'm saying all this because –'

'Because you might not come back,' Alice whispered into his chest, and closed her eyes again. 'Teddy?' she said.

'Mmmm?' he replied.

'I'm proud that you're my brother. And even

though I hate the war, I think you're brave to sign up. Sorry I was so cross about it.'

Teddy held her extra tightly. 'Thank you, Tink. That's a decent thing to say.'

'But Teddy?' she said. 'I still don't want you to leave. I want always to know where you are.'

Teddy brushed back his tumbly hair so that Alice could see right into his handsome face. 'You *will* know where I am. Because we'll be looking up at the very same moon. If you miss me, go to the window and look at the sky. I would have looked up at it not long before, and been thinking of you.'

'But what if you die?' asked Alice. 'How will you think of me then?'

'Not going to happen. I've too much to come home for.' Teddy was trying to sound brave, but Alice knew him too well to be fooled.

He didn't say anything else for a long time, just sat stroking her hair and looking out at the water, which was sparkling like a paddock of diamonds. Finally, he cleared his throat. 'Take care of them all for me.'

'I will. I'll do my super very best.'

'And Tink? I'd love to see you dance when you get home.' He raised his hand as she began to protest. 'I know you don't feel like it now. But just don't shut the door on it altogether. It's too important.' He kissed the top of her head. 'We should be going before the current gets too strong.'

They waded in and swam back together, the light dangling through the water like a net, Teddy's feet, like quick white fish, at the ends of her fingers, just out of reach.

When they were halfway there, Alice spotted a figure signalling frantically to them from the end of the jetty. As they got closer, she could see that it was Mabel. Alice stopped and waved, treading water and smiling.

But Mabel didn't smile back. 'Hurry *up*!' she shouted, her voice cracked through with panic. '*Please.* We've had a cablegram about Papa Sir.' She turned and ran, and as Alice churned through the shallows after Teddy, suddenly she felt that her legs couldn't kick, that her arms were damp string. Cablegrams didn't often bring good news. Please, Papa Sir, she thought with each stroke, please be all right.

By the time she got to shore, Teddy was waiting at the water's edge, his hand held out towards her.

'Teddy,' she said as she took it and ran with him up the sand. 'I'm frightened.'

'Me too,' said Teddy. 'But I'm here, Tink. I'm still with you.'

by Davina Bell

Like most Australian girls, my heritage is a patchwork of pieces from many places, stitched together by chance and love. My parents met on the ski slopes in Italy. Dad is Australian, but his ancestors include a pair of Italian apothecaries and an Irish minister, and he grew up in Singapore. My mother, who's English, went to a boarding school called Battle Abbey and was a nurse in a tiny African country called Lesotho, where she lived in a mud hut with a thatched roof.

I grew up in Perth, and on very hot days when I couldn't play outside, I'd sit and spin a globe for hours, waiting for the afternoon sea breeze and picturing life in those faraway places with their strange, lovely names. Perhaps all that imagining is what led me to be a writer.

HOW I BECAME AN AUSTRALIAN GIRL

by Lucia Masciullo

I was born and grew up in Italy, a beautiful country to visit, but also a difficult country to live in for new generations.

In 2006, I packed up my suitcase and I left Italy with the man I love. We bet on Australia. I didn't know much about Australia before coming – I was just looking for new opportunities, I guess.

And I liked it right from the beginning! Australian people are resourceful, open-minded and always with a smile on their faces. I think all Australians keep in their blood a bit of the pioneer heritage, regardless of their own birthplace.

Here I began a new life and now I'm doing what I always dreamed of: I illustrate stories. Here is the place where I'd like to live and to grow up my children, in a country that doesn't fear the future.

Alice's
Time

WORLD War One, sometimes called the Great War, went from 1914 to 1918. It began when Franz Ferdinand II – Archduke of the Austro-Hungarian Empire – was shot by a Serbian secret society, but really the causes were more complicated than that.

Lots of countries in Europe had been at war before, so they were already old friends or enemies. When Austria-Hungary declared war on Serbia, it was like the world split into teams based on the old agreements they had to protect each other: Germany and Austria-Hungary on one side; Britain, France and Russia on the other.

Because Australia had been settled by the British in 1788, most Australians still thought of themselves as part of the British Empire. So when England was drawn into the war, Australia followed.

For lots of young men, war was a chance to see the world, and to be adventurous and brave. No one imagined it would last very long.

Men and boys who didn't sign up to fight were seen as unpatriotic and some were sent white feathers in the mail, accusing them of being cowards. Receiving a feather was one of the most shameful things that could happen to a man, and disgraced his family, too.

Even though the war was being fought so far away, many worried about what would happen if Britain lost and Germany invaded Australia. This made them suspicious of people with German heritage (even those who had been born here) and that's why almost 7000 Australians with German backgrounds were put into prison camps during this time.

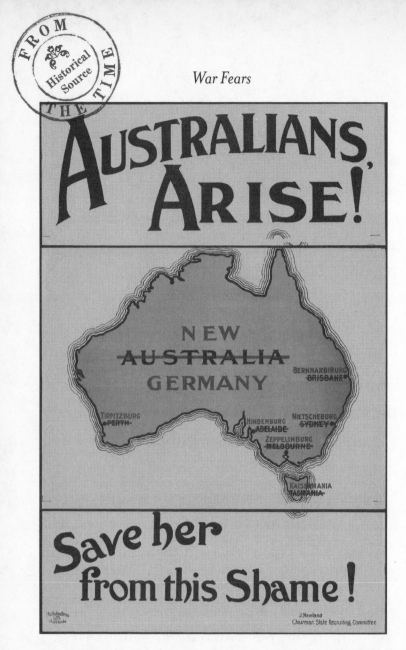

During World War One, there was a real fear in Australia that if Germany won the war, life would change forever in all sorts of terrible ways. Lots of posters and advertisements (like the one above) were made by the government to fuel this fear so that men would sign up to defend the country, and everyone would be united against the enemy.

DID YOU KNOW THAT IN 1918 . . .

The Spanish Influenza pandemic killed twenty-five million people in twenty-five weeks.

The Russian royal family was executed in Siberia.

A woman called Mammy Lou became the oldest person ever to star in a movie, aged 114.

In America, more than 100 waiters were arrested for putting a poisonous powder called 'Mickey Finn' into restaurant food.

Nelson Mandela was born in South Africa.

Civil War broke out in Russia.

Two classic Australian books were published: *Snugglepot and Cuddlepie* by May Gibbs and *The Magic Pudding* by Norman Lindsay.

100 million gramophone records were sold worldwide.

Constance Markiewicz became the first woman to be elected to parliament in the British House of Commons.

Australia's first electric train ran between Newmarket and Flemington Racecourse in Melbourne.

Want to find out more?

Turn the page for a
sneak peek at Book 2

Alice and the
Apple Blossom Fair

As Alice and Uncle Bear waited on the corner of the Perth–Fremantle Road to cross over to their favourite shops, Alice thought how much she loved the sounds of the Village, so different from home, though it was really only a short walk away. Home was the squabbling of Pudding's chickens, Honey's moo, the rustle of the river and the squeak of all the windmills over the water tanks; the sound of the gramophone and Mabel singing. But the Village was hooves clopping and people calling and the hoot of trains; it was naughty boys throwing stones, the hiss of the laundry, the tinkle of the bell that told them Jimmy Poor Eye was coming, pushing his cart with his special gadget that sharpened knives. It was the thrum of little motor cars and ladies chatting outside the post office, and Ford, the little station-master, blowing his whistle, the sound of the ice man's horse and cart, and the calls of the children from all the families that Alice had known forever. It was as if everything exciting about the world was right there in Napoleon Street, playing together like a thrilling piece of music.

Alice felt for Uncle Bear's hand and squeezed it. 'I'm glad I'm not going to go off and be a ballerina after all. I never want to live anywhere else but here.'

Uncle Bear looked down at her and raised his eyebrows, as if he didn't quite believe her. And as she looked into his clear blue eyes, she realised she didn't quite believe herself.

'Well, maybe it would have been nice, Uncle Bear . . . When I was bigger, perhaps.'

As the milkman's horse and cart tripped past them, Alice spotted the long red ponytail of her best friend Jilly. 'Uncle Bear, there's Jilly. JILLY! I wonder if she got my note. And is that . . . Douglas?'

Douglas was Jilly's biggest brother, and the one Alice liked the least. He'd been away at war for three years – maybe more. Douglas was sly, the kind of sly where the only time he was doing the right thing was when a grown-up was turning round to check. And he was mean. But just as Alice adored her own brother Teddy, Jilly thought Douglas was marvellous too.

Alice and Uncle Bear crossed over to where Douglas was sitting on a bench in his uniform smoking a hand-rolled cigarette, a stick propped up beside him. Jilly stood next to him, balancing paper bags from Muggeridge's grocer, smiling.

'Hi, Jilly. Hello, Douglas. Welcome home,' said Alice. 'Are you well?'

Douglas squinted one eye shut and looked her up and down in a way that made Alice feel as if she were standing in only her petticoat. Then he turned his head and blew smoke out of the corner of his mouth. His hair seemed an angrier red than Alice remembered. Against his pale, yellowy skin, his freckles stood out like the pattern on a tablecloth. 'Heard Teddy finally got the nerve to sign up. Only took him three years. Shameful.'

Alice bristled. If I were a cat right now, she thought, my claws would be out, and I'd slash him.

Meet the other Australian girls

Meet Nellie
1849

It's 1849 and Nellie O'Neill is arriving in South Australia on a ship bringing orphan girls from Irish workhouses. Nellie and her best friend, Mary, have left the famine in Ireland far behind, and are full of hopes and dreams for the future. Nellie longs to learn to read, to be part of a family once more, and never to be hungry again. But with no job and no one to turn to, how will Nellie's wishes come true?

Meet Nellie and join her adventure in the first of four exciting stories about an Irish girl with a big heart, in search of the freedom to be herself.

Penny Matthews, critically acclaimed author of the Nellie books, has written junior novels, chapter books, and picture books. Her novel, *A Girl Like Me*, was a CBCA Notable Book in 2010 and won the Sisters in Crime's 2011 Davitt Award for Young Adult Fiction.

GRACE
1808

It's 1808 and Grace is living with her uncle in London. They have no money, and Grace is always lonely and often hungry. One afternoon she can't resist taking a shiny red apple from a grocer's cart – and in a split second, her life changes forever...

You can read all the books in the Grace series...

MEET GRACE
A FRIEND FOR GRACE
GRACE AND GLORY
A HOME FOR GRACE

LETTY
1841

It's 1841 and Letty is on the docks in England, farewelling her bossy older sister who is about to take a long sea voyage to Australia. But then there's a mix-up and Letty finds herself on the ship too. How will she manage on the other side of the world, and what will life be like there?

You can read all the books in the Letty series...

MEET LETTY
LETTY AND THE STRANGER'S LACE
LETTY ON THE LAND
LETTY'S CHRISTMAS

Poppy
1864

It's 1864 and Poppy lives at Bird Creek
Mission near Echuca. When her brother,
Gus, runs away to pan for gold, Poppy
plans her own escape . . . Will she ever
find Gus, whom she loves more than
anything in the world?

You can read all the books in the Poppy series . . .

Meet Poppy
Poppy at Summerhill
Poppy and the Thief
Poppy Comes Home

Rose
1900

It's 1900 and Rose lives with her family
in a big house in Melbourne. She wants
to play cricket, climb trees and be an
adventurer. But Rose's mother has other
ideas. Will Rose ever really get
to do the things she loves?

You can read all the books in the Rose series . . .

Meet Rose
Rose on Wheels
Rose's Challenge
Rose in Bloom

ouraustraliangirl.com.au

Want to find out more?
To play games, enter competitions and read more
about your favourite characters, visit our website.
We'd love to hear from you!

Follow the story of your favourite
Australian girls and you will see that there
is a special charm on the cover of each book
that tells you something about the story.

Here they all are. You can tick them
off as you read each one.

Meet Grace

**A Friend
for Grace**

**Grace
and Glory**

**A Home
for Grace**

MEET LETTY

LETTY AND THE
STRANGER'S
LACE

LETTY
ON THE LAND

LETTY'S
CHRISTMAS

Meet Poppy

*Poppy at
Summerhill*

*Poppy and
the Thief*

*Poppy
Comes Home*

Meet Rose

Rose on Wheels

*Rose's
Challenge*

Rose in Bloom

Meet Nellie

Nellie and
the Secret Letter

Nellie's Quest

Nellie's
Greatest Wish

 ✓

Meet Alice

Alice and the
Apple Blossom Fair

Alice of
Peppermint Grove

Peacetime
for Alice

A girl like me in a time gone by